W9-ACS-036

Purchase of this book made possible
through a grant from the
Laura Bush Foundation for
America's Libraries.

THE LAURA BUSH FOUNDATION
FOR AMERICA'S LIBRARIES

Moxy Maxwell Does Not Love Writing Thank-you Notes

Moxy Maxwell Does Not Love Writing Thank-you Notes

By Peggy Gifford

Photographs by Valorie Fisher

schwartz & wade books · new york

Published in the United States by Schwartz & Wade Books, an imprint of
Random House Children's Books, a division of Random House, Inc., New York.

This is a work of fiction. Names, characters, places, and incidents either are the
product of the author's imagination or are used fictitiously. Any resemblance to
actual persons, living or dead, events, or locales is entirely coincidental.

Text copyright © 2008 by Peggy Gifford
Photographs copyright © 2008 by Valorie Fisher

All rights reserved.

Schwartz & Wade Books and colophon are trademarks of Random House, Inc.

Visit us on the Web! www.randomhouse.com/kids

Educators and librarians, for a variety of teaching tools, visit us at
www.randomhouse.com/teachers

Library of Congress Cataloging-in-Publication Data
Gifford, Peggy Elizabeth.
 Moxy Maxwell does not love writing thank-you notes / by Peggy Gifford ;
photographs by Valorie Fisher.
 p. cm.
 Summary: Ten-year-old Moxy Maxwell has promised to write twelve thank-you
notes by the day after Christmas so that she and her twin brother Mark can go
to Hollywood to visit their father, but all her brilliant ideas to help finish the
task more efficiently end up creating chaos in the house.
 ISBN 978-0-375-84270-2 (trade) — ISBN 978-0-375-94552-6 (lib. bdg.)
 [1. Thank-you notes—Fiction. 2. Behavior—Fiction. 3. Twins—Fiction.
4. Brothers and sisters—Fiction. 5. Family life—Fiction. 6. Christmas—Fiction.
7. Humorous stories.] I. Fisher, Valorie, ill. II. Title.

PZ7.G3635Mw 2008
[Fic]—dc22
 2007015686

The text of this book is set in Whitman.
Book design by Rachael Cole

Printed in the United States of America

10 9 8 7 6 5 4 3 2 1

First Edition

Random House Children's Books supports the First Amendment and
celebrates the right to read.

For Jack
—P.G.

For Harriet and Margret
—V.F.

Acknowledgments

I am indebted to Anne Schwartz, Lee Wade, and Valorie Fisher, whose talent and seamless collaboration made this book possible.

—P.G.

I would like to thank my exceptionally talented and hardworking cast of characters: Elinor, Charlie, Aidan, Olive, Anne, David, Matt, Buster, and Granny.

And I am enormously grateful to Peggy for her hilariously inspirational world of Moxy.

—V.F.

chapter 1
We Begin

It was the day after Christmas and Moxy Maxwell had a List of 13 Things to Do Before Tomorrow. Tomorrow she and her twin brother, Mark, were flying to Hollywood to spend the last week of vacation with their father.

Moxy had been looking forward to this trip for, as she put it, "ages and ages"—ever since her mother called her dad and told him that *this year* he *had* to take the twins for the last part of Christmas vacation.

Mark and Moxy's father's name was

Rock Hunter, and he was a Big Mover and Shaker out in Hollywood. But Moxy and Mark hadn't seen him for almost three years. Two years ago he canceled their Christmas visit at the last minute because he had to fly to the Dead Sea to help a Major Star who was having a breakdown on the set of a made-for-TV movie called *Noah's Wife: The Untold Story.* And last year he was so busy establishing himself in his new career as a Big Mover and Shaker in Hollywood that he had forgotten about Christmas altogether. But this year he was finally a Big Man Behind the Scenes out there.

"Behind the scenes is where the real action is" was what he'd told Moxy when she had asked why she'd never seen his picture in *People* magazine or *Us Weekly* magazine or *Star* magazine or any magazine.

chapter 2

Numbers 1 Through 12 on Moxy's List of 13 Things to Do Before Tomorrow

Numbers 1 through 12 on Moxy's List of 13 Things to Do Before Tomorrow were to write twelve thank-you notes. Last year she hadn't finished writing the thank-you notes for her Christmas presents until the day before Easter. This year, she promised her mother, they'd *all* be finished by the day *after* Christmas. And today was the day after Christmas.

"Dear Nonnie, Thank you for the fabulous money. Love, Me," read Moxy. She was resting on her bed, her new thank-you-note stationery balanced on her knees, while her mother folded Moxy's baby blue petal-patterned swim-suit into her suitcase.

"Tell Nonnie how you're going to spend the money," said Mrs. Maxwell. "And be sure to wish her a happy New Year."

"But that will take *forever*," said Moxy. "And I have eleven more thank-you notes to go."

"A thank-you note isn't something you *have to do*, it should *mean something*. It should come from your heart," said Mrs. Maxwell.

"But my heart hasn't got time," Moxy replied. "It has to go with my body to the mall to exchange the evening gown Aunt Margaret and I picked out for me to wear to the Big New Year's Eve Star-Studded Hollywood Bash Dad's taking me and Mark to. He said Madonna might even be there."

"I heard Shrek might be there too," said Mark. Mark wasn't "thrilled to death" (as Moxy put it) about the Big New Year's Eve Star-Studded Hollywood Bash.

Not only was Mark Maxwell the second-most-famous photographer on Palmetto Lane, he was also packed for their trip tomorrow, which was why he had time to take this picture of the inside of Moxy's half-packed suitcase. He called it "California Dreamin'."

"California Dreamin'," by Mark Maxwell.

Exchanging the evening gown Moxy and Aunt Margaret had picked out for Moxy to wear was number 13 on Moxy's List of 13 Things to Do Before Tomorrow.

chapter 3
5 Reasons Why Moxy Had to Exchange the Evening Gown

1. It was strapless.

2. It was black.

3. It had too many sequins.

4. It had a train that extended five feet behind her.

5. Moxy was only ten.

"It's a shame it didn't work out," said Moxy. She was looking at the photograph Mark had taken of her when she first modeled the dress for everyone. He called it "Moxy's Moxie."

"Moxy's Moxie," by Mark Maxwell.

"I'm sure we'll find something just as cute at the mall this afternoon," Moxy went on. "I think I'll go with a short skirt this time—something with gobs of glitter."

"You're not going with anything, including with me to the mall, until you finish writing your thank-you notes," said Mrs. Maxwell. She was looking under Moxy's bed as she spoke. She pulled out two old ice cream bowls and a plate with a fork stuck to it.

"Mom, have you decided where you want to live when I'm a rich and famous movie star and buy you a mansion?" asked Moxy, gazing at the big toe on her left foot. (It looked bigger than usual.)

Number 3 on Moxy's List of 218 Possible Career Paths was to become a rich and famous movie star and adopt 17 starving children from around the world (she wasn't sure if she would have a husband) and live with them and their 17 nannies in a mansion near all the other rich and famous movie stars who were adopting starving children from around the world.

Moxy had been studying how to break into show business for more than three weeks now, and as far as she could tell there were only two ways to do it. One way was to have enormous talent and perseverance. The other way was to be "discovered." Being "discovered" seemed easier.

But according to Moxy's father, the only way to be "discovered" was to be seen around "the scene," which was why this trip to Hollywood was so important.

The way Moxy figured it, all that stood between her and a three-movie deal was twelve thank-you notes.

chapter 4
In Which Mrs. Maxwell Begins a Sentence with "If you don't stop dreaming and start writing your thank-you notes right now . . ."

"**If you don't** stop dreaming and start writing your thank-you notes right now, there are going to be consequences," said Mrs. Maxwell.

chapter 5
A Brief Word About the Word "Consequences"

August 23 had been the third-worst day of Moxy's life (for details see *Moxy Maxwell Does Not Love* Stuart Little, pages 1–92). Ever since then, Moxy had paid very close attention when her mother used the word "consequences."

In case you don't know, consequences are what happen when you don't do *exactly*, *precisely*, and *specifically* what your mother tells you to do. In Moxy's limited experience, consequences had never been a good thing. In fact, "consequences" was the only twelve-letter word that made Moxy feel like she might collapse.

"Since you want to know," said Moxy, "the real problem with my new thank-you notes—and thank you very much for them, by the way—is that they already say 'Thank You' in big gold letters across the front, and what is the point of writing 'thank you' inside when 'thank you' is already written outside?

"It doesn't leave much to write about," she added.

chapter 6
In Which Mark Says Something

"Just write the notes, Moxy," said Mark. He was looking through his camera's viewfinder at the maple tree that he and Ajax, his stepfather, had wrapped in little white twinkling lights on the first day of Christmas vacation.

chapter 7
In Which Moxy Has a Really Good Idea (Really)

"Mom, I just had a really good idea," said Moxy, ignoring (and not for the first time) her brother. "What I'm going to do is write my thank-you notes while I'm in Hollywood."

She could just picture herself sitting by the pool in her baby blue petal-patterned swimsuit with her red heart-shaped sunglasses, writing thank-you notes. "That way I can wish everyone a happy New Year and get a tan at the same time."

Moxy also liked the fact that she would be able to start every note with "Salutations from Hollywood." "Salutations" had the advantage of being an eleven-letter word, which meant it would take up more space than plain old four-lettered "Dear."

Besides, everyone would know she was visiting her father. She didn't care whether everyone knew she was visiting her father. Except that she sort of did. Practically everyone in the Northern Hemisphere knew she hadn't seen him in almost three years.

"What are you doing?" asked Mrs. Maxwell.

"Packing my thank-you-note stuff," said Moxy.

chapter 8
In Which Pansy Begins to Cry

Pansy, who was Moxy's little sister, and only five, was lying under Moxy's bed practicing to be a turtle—which was what she wanted to be when she grew up. (Mark wanted to be a photographer—which he already was—and Moxy was still considering which of 218 Possible Career Paths she would follow.)

Mrs. Maxwell lifted the bedspread and peered at her youngest child.

"Why are you crying, darling?"

"I want to go to Hollywood with Moxy and Mark."

Mrs. Maxwell lay down on the floor, pressed her left cheek against the exact spot on the carpet where Moxy had accidentally spilled a jar of the perfume she had invented on the second day of Christmas vacation, and looked into Pansy's eyes.

"What's that smell?" said Mrs. Maxwell.

"Do you like it?" exclaimed Moxy. "It's a product I've been developing for my new Moxy Maxwell Socks and Scents collection."

Pansy stopped crying and started sniffing the floor.

"I call it Eau de Moxy," said Moxy modestly.

"What's it made of?" asked Pansy.

"It's a surprising combination of household products and three kinds of perfume."

Mrs. Maxwell got up. There followed a brief exchange between Moxy and her mother, the details of which I won't go into. (It is enough to say that the words "Pine-Sol" and "Lemon Pledge" were mentioned.)

But if I stop and tell you every detail of every conversation, I'll never get back to the question before us, which is why Pansy couldn't go to Hollywood with Mark and Moxy.

The reason Pansy couldn't go to Hollywood was that she had a different father than Mark and Moxy.

chapter 9
Divorce and the Problem of Last Names

When Mark and Moxy were quite young (Moxy had just started to walk and Mark had just started to read), their father moved to New York City to star as a character named Dr. Flint Stone on the TV show *As the World Twirls*. Unfortunately, Dr. Flint Stone had contracted a severe case of malaria while he was in Africa looking for a kidnapped nurse, and he hadn't survived the first season. But Moxy's father decided to stay in New York anyway, even though he no longer had a job, and Moxy's mother decided to stay in Ohio, and they decided to get a divorce.

A few years later, during Story Hour at the local library, Moxy's mother was "swept off her feet" (Moxy's words) by the famous children's poet A. Jackson Maxwell (Mark and Moxy call him Ajax). And after a "whirlwind romance" (Moxy again), they were married.

There was, however, considerable confusion about how someone named Mrs. *Maxwell* could be the mother of two children named Mark and Moxy *Hunter,* and how Mark and Moxy *Hunter* could have a sister named Pansy *Maxwell.*

Finally, they all agreed to choose just one name for everyone.

"Maxwell" won by just one vote.

chapter 10
60 Words About Mark and Moxy's Stepfather, Ajax

Ajax wrote children's books all day (and sometimes right through dinner and sometimes he was still writing children's books when Pansy went to bed and sometimes he was still writing children's books when Mark and Moxy went to bed— although Moxy didn't really go to sleep when she went to bed, she read books under the covers with her flashlight).

chapter 11
2:01 p.m.—In Which Moxy Looks at Her Clock

"Mom, shouldn't we be going to the mall soon?" Moxy was looking at her clock. It said 2:01 p.m.

"*I'm* going to the mall as soon as I take these dirty dishes downstairs," said Mrs. Maxwell. "*You're* going to the mall as soon as you finish writing your thank-you notes."

"But you'll be downstairs before I can even get started."

"Then I guess you're not going to the mall."

Moxy was shocked. "But I have to exchange my evening gown!"

But Mrs. Maxwell was already walking down the stairs. She was also calling Uncle Jayne on her cell phone. She was also carrying two old ice cream bowls and a plate with a fork stuck to it *and* Moxy's black evening gown. (Over the years Moxy had observed that a really first-rate mother can do many things at once without messing any of them up.)

Moxy listened as she followed her mother down the stairs.

"Uncle Jayne? . . . Well, Merry Christmas to you too," said Mrs. Maxwell—even though Christmas was yesterday. "Would you mind coming over to sit with the children while I dash to the mall?"

Apparently Uncle Jayne didn't mind, because Mrs. Maxwell was saying "thank you" by the time she reached the bottom stair. She was moving so rapidly that Mark, who was behind Moxy, couldn't even get a photograph of her.

chapter 12
Introducing
Granny George

They found Granny George sitting in the kitchen, knitting a shocking-pink bonnet for covering up toilet paper. She was going to sell it at the annual Save the Ivory-billed Woodpecker Fund-raiser.

(Even though Granny George officially lived in Arizona, she spent her winters in Ohio visiting the Maxwells. Granny George didn't like warm winters.)

Here's a picture Mark took of Granny George knitting the shocking-pink bonnet for covering up toilet paper.

*Granny George's legs.**

You probably can't tell from the photograph, but Mudd, who was one of the Maxwells' dogs, had been playing ball all morning with Granny George's ball of shocking-pink yarn.

After Mark took this picture of part of Granny George's legs, Mrs. Maxwell suggested that he help Granny George roll the ball of shocking-pink yarn back into a ball.

*Granny George's legs are featured here wearing socks from the new Moxy Maxwell Socks and Scents collection.

Actually, it was more than a suggestion—it had a "do it now" flavor.

So Mark put his camera down and started rolling up the yarn.

chapter 13
Why Moxy Maxwell Does Not Love Crafts

Even though Granny George loved crafts and was excellent at them, Moxy hated them. This was because crafts usually involved white paste that didn't stick and round scissors that didn't cut and construction paper that felt dry and very unpleasant under your fingertips.

Moxy *did* like spray paint, though. Unfortunately she wasn't allowed to touch another can of it until she was twenty-one years old.

For Christmas, Granny George had given Moxy a pencil holder made from an empty can of peas and decorated with glued-on macaroni. It was spray-painted gold.

Here is a close-up photograph Mark took on Christmas morning of the gold pencil holder with the glued-on macaroni Granny George had made for Moxy. He called it "Where the Peas Were."

"Where the Peas Were," by Mark Maxwell.

It occurred to Moxy that if she thanked Granny George for the pencil holder right now, she might not have to write a thank-you note to her later.

"Granny George, thank you for the pencil holder," said Moxy. She leaned down and kissed the top of Granny George's head.

"Pencil holder?" said Granny George. Sometimes Granny George had a problem with remembering.

chapter 14
In Which Mrs. Maxwell Says, "Come into the hall this minute, young lady."

"Come into the hall this minute, young lady," said Mrs. Maxwell.

Moxy went into the hall that minute.

"I heard you say thank you to Granny George just now, which was very nice of you. But you still have to write her a thank-you note."

"But she doesn't even remember she gave it to me," said Moxy.

"Last Easter you promised me that all of your thank-you notes would be done by the day after Christmas," said Mrs. Maxwell, ignoring Moxy's last remark.

"But last Easter I didn't know I'd be getting ready to go to Hollywood."

"As far as I can see, you're not getting ready to go to Hollywood now. You're not writing your thank-you notes either. You're not even listening to me tell you to write thank-you notes. What exactly *are* you doing?"

"I must be thinking," said Moxy.

chapter 15
In Which Mrs. Maxwell Gives Moxy One More Thing to Think About (As If Moxy Didn't Have Enough on Her Mind)

"Well, think about this," said Mrs. Maxwell. "If you haven't finished your thank-you notes by the time I get back from the mall, you're not going to Hollywood to see your father."

As soon as she saw the expression on Moxy's face, Mrs. Maxwell knew she had gone too far. And even though she suspected that Moxy knew she hadn't really meant it, Mrs. Maxwell was sorry she had said it.

"You're just jealous because I'm going to see Dad!" cried Moxy.

Mrs. Maxwell didn't even have to say "Go to your room, young lady," because Moxy had already run up the stairs.

chapter 16

In Which
Mrs. Maxwell's
1989 Volvo DL
with the Three
New Tires
and the 2002
Transmission
and the Once-Heated
Seats
and the Broken
Back Windshield Wiper
Vibrates
down the Driveway

Moxy and Pansy listened as Mrs. Maxwell's 1989 Volvo DL vibrated down the driveway. (*She really should get a new muffler,* thought Moxy, *if not for the environment, then for me.*)

Then Pansy stuck her head out from under the bed. "Are we *alone*?" she asked.

"Uncle Jayne will be here any minute. I heard Mom call him," said Moxy.

Pansy pulled her head back under the bed and stuck her feet out the other end. Her sneakers were untied. Pansy had been learning to tie her shoes since last June. It was a complicated maneuver.

"If I don't finish my thank-you notes by the time Mom gets home, I can't go visit my dad in Hollywood," moaned Moxy.

Then she lay down on the bed, looked over at the picture of her father she always kept on her dresser, and put three pillows over her face.

Here is Mark's photograph of the photograph of their dad Moxy always kept on her dresser.

For those of you who can't read what
their dad wrote on the front, it says:
    Especially for Mark & Moxy
    Best Wishes
    from
    Rock Hunter

chapter 17
In Which (Quite Unexpectedly) Pansy Makes a Wise, Though Somewhat Muffled, Suggestion

"I'll tell your thank-you notes to you out loud and you write down what I say," said Pansy. "It'll be a snap."

"Snap" was Pansy's new favorite word. She had learned it when she learned about snapping turtles—something she most certainly was not going to be when she grew up. She was going to be an Eastern box turtle.

But Moxy could barely hear her, so she took the three pillows off her face and stuck her head under the bed.

"What did you say?" said Moxy.

Pansy was wearing black tights and a matching black leotard—the same outfit (as Pansy had explained more than once) turtles wear under their shells.

"I'll tell your thank-you notes to you out loud and you write down what I say," repeated Pansy—only this time she spoke ve-ry slow-ly, like turtles do.

Moxy stuffed the three pillows behind her back and leaned against the headboard. It was her most natural thinking position.

Pansy's idea appealed to her one hun-dred percent. It meant she wouldn't have to do all the work herself.

"Just write down what I say," instructed Pansy.

chapter 18
Moxy Gets Organized

But then Moxy couldn't find her thank-you notes, so she had to grope around the bed for them. She finally located them on the other side of her suitcase. Then Moxy couldn't find a pen. Then Moxy found a pen *without the cap on* in her suitcase next to her off-white cropped pants (which she was going to wear on her second day in Hollywood).

Then Moxy couldn't find her List of 12 People to Write Thank-you Notes To.

"Where's my List of Twelve People to Write Thank-you Notes To?" she asked.

Pansy stuck her head out from under the bed and said, "I have it."

Moxy took the list and read the second name aloud. "I got bubble bath from Mrs. Button White." She squinted as she read.

Even though the eye doctor had told Mrs. Maxwell that Moxy had perfect vision, Moxy was practicing squinting for when she was older. There was a girl at her school—a sixth grader named Valorie Pine—who squinted. Moxy watched her at recess and thought she looked very cute when she did it.

"You mean Mrs. Button White, the professional dog walker?" asked Pansy.

Moxy nodded.

"She didn't give *me* a present."

"You should take more of an interest in her career," replied Moxy.

Pansy mulled that over.

"Dear Mrs. Button White," Pansy finally said.

"Dear Mrs. Button White," wrote Moxy.

"Thank you for the bubble bath. Someday I will take a bath." Pansy paused to consider what to say next. "And I'm sorry your cat wandered away on the Fourth of July. Love, Moxy."

Just as she was writing "Dear Mrs. Button White," Moxy had a brilliant-beyond-belief idea.

chapter 19
Moxy's Brilliant-
Beyond-Belief Idea

It occurred to Moxy that she could write "Dear" and "Love, Moxy" on all 12 of her thank-you notes *right now* and fill in the middle part later. At least it would get her going.

Then she had an even more brilliant idea. It was such an incredibly good idea that Moxy insisted I call the next chapter "The Genius of Moxy."

chapter 20
The Genius of Moxy

"You know," said Moxy, "why should I even write 'Dear' and 'Love, Moxy' over and over again? It'll take an ice age."

Pansy stuck her head back under the bed.

"What I'll do is write 'Dear' and 'Love, Moxy' and 'Thank you for whatever' on just one note. Then I'll make twelve copies of it on the new copier Ajax got for Christmas and fill in the rest later."

chapter 21

The Sample Thank-you Note Moxy Wrote to Copy on Ajax's New Copier (Which He Just Got from Mrs. Maxwell for Christmas, by the Way)

This is what Moxy wrote:

Dear_____,

    Thank you for _____. It is very_____and it will come in handy. I'll use it for various things like _____ and _____. In case you want to thank me for this thank you note, please wait until I get back from visiting my dad in Hollywood. I will be there for 6½ days.

    Have a breath-taking New Year!

    Love,

    Moxy Anne Maxwell

chapter 22
In Which Mark Happens to Wander by Moxy's Room and Say "I wouldn't use Ajax's new copier if I were you."

All this time, Mark was following Granny George up and down the hall outside Moxy's room. He was carrying her ball of shocking-pink yarn because he was afraid she'd drop it again. (Granny George liked to walk and knit at the same time).

"I wouldn't use Ajax's new copier if I were you," he called out as he passed Moxy's door for the eleventh time.

"Me neither," added Pansy. But Moxy couldn't hear her because Pansy's head was still under her bed.

"I'll write my own thank-you note," Granny George called out without missing a stitch. The thing about Granny George was that just when you thought she was having trouble remembering, you discovered she completely got it. If Moxy hadn't been so comfortable, she would have jumped up and kissed her.

"Keep it simple," instructed Moxy. "Write 'Thank you for the pencil holder' and tell what I'm going to do with it—say something like 'I'll use it to hold my pencils.' Oh, and wish yourself a breathtaking New Year."

"Pencil holder?" said Granny George.

chapter 23

In Which the Author Offers 5 Reasons Why It Might Not Be a Good Idea for Moxy to Use Ajax's New Christmas Copier

1. The copier cost a ton of money.

2. The copier was brand-new.

3. Ajax loved the copier almost as much as he loved Mrs. Maxwell (at least, that's what he said when he opened it).

4. No one but Ajax was supposed to touch the copier (at least, that's what he said when he opened it).

5. Moxy had never run a copier before.

chapter 24
In Which Moxy Offers 3 Reasons Why It Is a Good Idea to Use Ajax's New Christmas Copier

1. Mark is a genius at making things like copiers work.

2. I really need it.

3. Ajax isn't home.

Moxy jammed a fourth pillow behind her back. She was not tired, exactly—she was tired inexactly.

"Mark," she said, "go warm up Ajax's new copier." She thought about it and patched a "please" onto the end.

Mark considered his options. Granny George was almost done knitting her toilet paper bonnet, which meant his hands would soon be free of the ball of shocking-pink yarn.

But the thing was, Mark preferred taking pictures of Moxy getting into trouble rather than actually helping Moxy get into trouble.

chapter 25
In Which Mark Says No

"No."

chapter 26

In Which Moxy's Cell Phone Plays the First Two Notes of Beethoven's Fifth Symphony

Moxy was so quick on the draw when she picked up her cell phone that Ajax often remarked that she would have made a first-rate gunslinger in the Old West. And this time was no exception.

After the second but before the third note of Beethoven's Fifth Symphony, Moxy was saying "Yes" into the phone. "Yes" was what Moxy said instead of "Hello," unless it was someone she didn't know.

Mark took these three blurry photo-graphs of Moxy as she picked up her cell

A step-by-step illustration of Moxy's Rapid Cell-Phone-Answering Technique.

phone so you can study her technique. (He used really, really, really high-speed film. You'll have to ask him for sure, but I think it was going at least a thousand miles per hour.)

It was Sam on the other end of the phone. Sam lived at 8 Palmetto Lane, which was only 7 houses from Moxy's house, and even though he was only six, he was Moxy's best friend. He would do anything for her.

"Sam," said Moxy. "Please come over here ASAP and warm up Ajax's new copier. I'm going to make copies of my thank-you note so I won't have to write 'Dear' and 'Love, Moxy' twelve hundred thousand times."

"How many thank-you notes have you written so far?" asked Sam. (Sam always kept track of Moxy.)

"Well, Granny George said she'd write her own note, but I'm not absolutely positively sure she will, and Mrs. Button White's is *somewhat* done, and Nonnie's needs a quick rewrite. So I guess I still have twelve thank-you notes to go."

"I don't know how to turn a copier on," said Sam. He hated to disappoint Moxy.

"All you have to do is press the On button," replied Moxy. She was starting to run out of patience.

"I'll be right over," said Sam.

chapter 27
In Which Rosie and Mudd Start Barking Like Mad Dogs

Then Rosie and Mudd started barking like mad dogs.

Rosie and Mudd were the Maxwells' dogs. Mudd, whom you've already met, belonged to Moxy. He was part black Lab, part German shepherd, and part himself. Rosie was a cute little white terrier with a bad attitude and a big blue bow on her head.

"Someone better answer the door," called out Moxy.

"Mark, answer the door." Moxy could be a little bossy.

"You answer it. I'm holding a ball of yarn."

Moxy leaned over and lifted the bedspread. "Pansy, please answer the door," she said.

"All right, but it'll take a long time. Turtles are slow."

chapter 28
In Which Moxy Comments That She Is the Only One Who Ever Does Anything Around Here

Moxy sighed rather loudly. "Has anyone noticed that I'm the only one who ever does anything around here?" she said.

There was a general silence.

Then slowly, so as not to strain herself, Moxy got off her bed, padded over to her bedroom window, and opened it. Snow spilled off the ledge and onto the carpet.

"Ho! Ho! Ho! Merry Christmas!"

Uncle Jayne was standing in the front yard dressed like Santa Claus. His arms were full of presents.

"I'll be right down," shouted Moxy. She

closed the window. "It's Uncle Jayne and he's wearing a Santa suit."

Here's a photograph Mark took from Moxy's window of Uncle Jayne standing in the snow dressed like Santa Claus. Mark called this picture "Miraculously, Santa Claus and Uncle Jayne Arrive at the Same Time."

"Miraculously, Santa Claus and Uncle Jayne Arrive at the Same Time," by Mark Maxwell.

Moxy adored Uncle Jayne. Uncle Jayne could talk like a duck. He could touch his nose with the tip of his tongue. He could pull a quarter out of your ear. He could do anything.

As soon as Moxy got downstairs and opened the front door, she said, "Uncle Jayne, do you know how to turn on a copier?"

Uncle Jayne took off his Santa hat when he came in—he had extremely good manners. Then he gave Moxy a Christmas present wrapped in silver paper with a quite big, very fresh-looking red bow on top. Moxy could tell it was a professional wrap job. You couldn't even see the Scotch tape.

It occurred to her that this might mean another thank-you note. "But Christmas was yesterday," said Moxy.

"That's what I told your aunt Margaret. But she didn't have time for Christmas yesterday," said Uncle Jayne. Aunt Margaret was a rocket scientist.

chapter 29
In Which Pansy Without Her Shell and Mark and Granny George and Mudd and Rosie Come Downstairs to Wish Uncle Jayne a Merry Christmas

Granny George was the first to arrive. "Merry Christmas, son," she said, even though Uncle Jayne wasn't her son.

Pansy was the last to arrive. She bumped down the stairs on all fours, looking remarkably like a turtle without a shell.

Mark took this picture of her:

Pansy arrives, looking remarkably like a turtle without a shell.

"Would you be terribly hurt if I asked you to take my present back home?" Moxy said to Uncle Jayne.

Uncle Jayne looked confused.

"The problem is I already have twelve thank-you notes to write, and if I don't finish them by the time Mom gets back from the mall, she won't let me go to Hollywood and see my dad, and then I'll never be discovered and become a rich and famous movie star and adopt seventeen starving children from around the world and live in the same neighborhood as all the other rich and famous movie stars who adopt starving children from around the world."

Uncle Jayne looked concerned. "That does sound like cruel and unusual punishment," he said.

Moxy liked the sound of the phrase "cruel and unusual punishment" very much. She repeated it twice to herself so she'd remember it in the unlikely event her mother got home before she finished writing her thank-you notes.

"Not going to Hollywood isn't the worst thing that could happen," said Mark.

"Mark, he's our father, for goodness' sake, and we haven't seen him in almost three years."

"Exactly," replied Mark.

"Exactly what?" said Moxy.

"If he's our father, why *haven't* we seen him in almost three years?"

chapter 30
In Which Moxy Brings Mark Up to Speed Regarding the Situation Between Their Father and Noah's Wife

Mark and Moxy had gone over this before.

"You know very well Dad had to fly to the Dead Sea two Christmases ago to help that Big Star who was having a nervous breakdown on the set of *Noah's Wife: The Untold Story.*"

"Just one question, Moxy," said Mark. "Where *is Noah's Wife*?"

"Noah's wife? She's been dead for like five thousand years."

"I mean the *movie*. Have you seen it? Have you even seen previews for it?"

"A Big Hollywood Star whose name Dad can't reveal promised that the second he finished filming *Genesis*—his big new movie—he'd help *Noah's Wife* get the attention it deserves."

"Whatever," said Mark.

Moxy paused. She wondered if that Big Hollywood Star would be at the Big New Year's Eve Star-Studded Hollywood Bash her dad was taking them to, which reminded her that she had to write her thank-you notes—and soon!

chapter 31
In Which Moxy Says, and Not for the First Time in Her Life, "Everybody follow me!"

"Everybody follow me to Ajax's new Christmas copy machine!" Moxy called out. And everybody did.

Pansy followed Moxy, and Uncle Jayne followed Pansy, and Mark followed Uncle Jayne, and Granny George followed Mark.

Because Ajax was a famous children's book writer (as those of you who have not been skipping around in the story already know), his office was what Mrs. Maxwell called "a big mess." Ajax, however, called it "a medium-size mess" and sometimes "a normal-size mess."

There were 1,122 books on his book-shelves. Mark counted them on the third day of Christmas vacation because he was bored. Twenty-one of the books had been written by Ajax himself. There were also eleven piles of Important Papers sitting on the floor.

"Please wipe your feet," Moxy said to Uncle Jayne.

Uncle Jayne stomped—*one, two*—his big Santa boots on Ajax's rug, spattering ice and snow across the room.

Then Rosie and Mudd began to bark.

"That's got to be Sam—will someone *please* answer the door?"

But no one moved.

chapter 32
In Which Moxy Sighs Rather Loudly

Moxy sighed rather loudly and said, "Has anyone noticed that I'm the only one who ever does anything around here?"

There was a general silence.

But it turned out Moxy didn't have to go all the way back down the wet hall and open the very heavy front door with the wreath that fell off every time you opened or closed it, because Sam had already let himself in.

"Merry Christmas, Moxy," he said. He was standing at the threshold of Ajax's office. A small present was balanced on his somewhat wet right red mitten—you could definitely see the Scotch tape.

Here's a picture Mark took of Sam's somewhat wet right red mitten holding the Christmas present Sam had wrapped for Moxy. Mark called it "A Study in Scotch Tape."

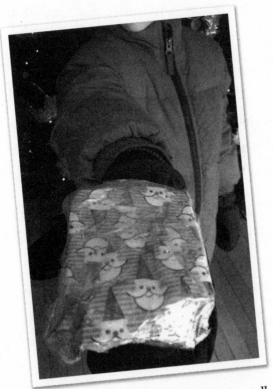

"A Study in Scotch Tape," by Mark Maxwell.

Everybody moved farther into Ajax's study so Sam could squeeze in.

"If that present's for me," said Moxy, "I don't want it."

Uncle Jayne looked surprised, and it occurred to Moxy that she was being, as her mother might say, the slightest bit rude.

"It'll mean one more thank-you note I have to write," she explained. "Maybe you can give it to me for my half birthday." Moxy always celebrated her half birthday, which was May 18. It broke up the year.

Then she climbed onto Ajax's La-Z-Boy chair and clapped her hands. "Listen up, everybody!" she called out. "To your right is Ajax's copier."

The copier was quite large. Quite hard to miss.

"What we're looking for," shouted

Moxy—she had to shout because everyone was talking at once, which was quite rude of them—"are the directions to the copier so that we can turn it on and make twelve copies of my sample thank-you note."

chapter 33
In Which Mark Maxwell Accidentally Backs into Ajax's Copier and Turns It On

The room was pretty crowded, what with Uncle Jayne and Pansy and Moxy and Granny George and Sam all trying to help, so when Mark backed up to get a picture, he accidentally backed into Ajax's new Christmas copier and turned it on.

You could tell it was on because 27 lights suddenly lit up (Mark counted them) and the machine made a sound like it was eating something. It was very surprising.

"Thank you, Mark!" Moxy called out. She had known all along that Mark would come through.

chapter 34
Moxy's Well-
Deserved Rest

"Does anyone know how to push this back?" Moxy was fooling around with the lever on Ajax's La-Z-Boy chair.

"I do," said Uncle Jayne. "Just lean forward."

"Forward?" said Moxy. "But I'm trying to go back."

Uncle Jayne pulled a Susan B. Anthony silver dollar out of Moxy's left ear and put it in her hand. It occurred to Moxy that she might have to write a thank-you note for it.

"Please put it back," she said.

Uncle Jayne put the silver dollar back in Moxy's left ear.

Moxy pushed her head as hard as she could against the back of Ajax's chair and tugged on the lever at the same time. Then there was the sound of something sort of breaking, or, as Moxy explained to her mother later, "the perfectly normal sound of a chair leaning back."

In any case, Ajax's La-Z-Boy flew all the way back and Moxy found that she was staring at the ceiling.

The ceiling could use a coat of paint, thought Moxy.

chapter 35
In Which Moxy Announces That It's Time to Get Organized

"People!" shouted Moxy. "It's time to get organized. Would someone please get the sample thank-you note I wrote so we can copy it?"

"I have it," said Pansy, who had been carrying it around.

chapter 36
In Which Uncle Jayne's Cell Phone Plays the Entire First Verse of "Santa Claus Is Coming to Town"

Uncle Jayne's phone went off.

It got as far as "He knows if you've been bad or good" before he could wrestle open the big hooks on his Santa Claus jacket, pull the phone out, and answer it.

"Darling," he said into the phone. Uncle Jayne was always calling Aunt Margaret darling, even though they'd been married for almost fifty-one thousand years.

chapter 37
In Which We Learn That Uncle Jayne's Christmas Turkey Has Finally Thawed and He Has to Dash Home and Pop It in the Oven, but He'll Be Right Back

It turned out Uncle Jayne's Christmas turkey had finally thawed and he had to dash home and pop it in the oven.

"But I'll be right back," promised Uncle Jayne.

Even Moxy understood why he had to go. Clearly Aunt Margaret couldn't put the turkey in. Ages and ages ago (back when Moxy was nine), Aunt Margaret had put the turkey in for Thanksgiving dinner and accidentally set the oven on self-clean instead of 325 degrees. And despite the fact that she had let the turkey self-clean itself for almost eleven hours, it had never turned golden brown—it had turned more blue-gray.

In the end they'd eaten frozen lasagna with cranberry sauce and pumpkin pie (which Moxy's mother had brought over). Uncle Jayne said it was without a doubt the best Thanksgiving dinner he'd ever had.

"But, Uncle Jayne, where am I supposed to put the thank-you note I want copied?" asked Moxy.

Uncle Jayne's rented Santa Claus boots were very big—size 13½, even though his regular shoes are size 10½—and Ajax's study was very small and crowded (as I've mentioned), which is why it wasn't Uncle Jayne's fault when he kicked over a small—thirty-nine-inch-tall—pile of Ajax's Important Papers as he walked over to the copier.

"It was an accident waiting to happen," Moxy said later to her mother.

Unfortunately, Moxy couldn't help Uncle Jayne pick up the Important Papers because she was having trouble getting out of Ajax's chair. She couldn't seem to get it back to a normal sitting position.

"As long as you're not hurt, it's perfectly all right," Moxy reassured poor Uncle Jayne, who was apologizing and picking up Important Papers at the same time.

On the next page is a photograph Mark took of Uncle Jayne on Ajax's Important Papers. Mark called it "Big Feet."

"Big Feet," by Mark Maxwell.

chapter 38
In Which Moxy and Uncle Jayne Have the Same Exact Thought at the Same Exact Time

Uncle Jayne slid over to the big copier. As he approached, he thought, *It looks like the cockpit of a jumbo jet.*

It looks like the cockpit of a jumbo jet, thought Moxy as Uncle Jayne approached the big copier, which reminded her that tomorrow at this time she would be landing in Hollywood. Unless, of course . . .

chapter 39
In Which Moxy
Thinks
the Unthinkable

. . . **unless, of course,** she didn't get her thank-you notes done.

chapter 40

In Which Uncle Jayne Finds the Place on the Copier Where Moxy's Sample Thank-you Note Should Go So It Can Be Copied

Uncle Jayne carefully arranged Moxy's sample thank-you note facedown on the copier so that Moxy—well, probably not Moxy—so that whoever Moxy told to make copies could make copies.

"Just punch in the number of copies you want and push Start," said Uncle Jayne.

The only way Moxy could think of to get out of Ajax's chair was to stand on one of the arms and jump.

But Moxy wasn't in the mood to jump.

Perhaps it was the position she'd been in—practically lying down. Perhaps it was exhaustion from all the thinking she'd been doing. But the only thing Moxy felt like doing was taking a nap.

Then she yawned—a great big delightful full-mouth sort of yawn.

"Sam? Pansy? Are you paying attention to what Uncle Jayne is telling you?" Moxy called out. "We have to be sure we understand what to do next."

"Make sure you have enough paper," said Uncle Jayne. He looked at the paper trays. There were five, and each one had a stack of different-colored paper on it. (Ajax was very fond of colored copy paper.) Uncle Jayne estimated that there were about 100 sheets of each color, which added up to about 500 pieces of paper altogether.

"You have enough paper," declared Uncle Jayne.

But Moxy's eyes were already closed.

"Should we wake her up?" asked Pansy.

"Not a good idea," replied Sam.

Waking Moxy when she was in the middle of a dream was a dangerous thing. That was because Moxy loved to dream almost as much as she loved to be awake.

Just then she was dreaming she was Eleanor Roosevelt, and—as Moxy would be the first to tell you—that's exactly the sort of dream that only happens once—twice at most—in a lifetime.

"Press this big red button," Uncle Jayne said to those of us who were still awake, "and huggaly-puggaly-smuggaly-smote, you'll have copies of Moxy's thank-you note!"

Then he pulled the Susan B. Anthony silver dollar he had put back in Moxy's left ear out of Pansy's right ear and gave it to her.

"I'll be right back," he said, and walked out the door.

chapter 41
In Which Pansy Pushes the Big Red Start Button Before Sam Is Ready

Sam punched "12" into the copier. But the number didn't show up in the little box. So he pressed "12" again. Nothing. Once more, he pressed "12," and just as he did, he noticed he'd been looking for the "12" in the wrong little box. The right little box said "121,212."

chapter 42
The Really Big Mess Begins

At that exact moment, Pansy pushed the big red Start button. Sam hadn't yet figured out how to change the number of copies from 121,212 back to 12. If he had, this story wouldn't be quite as good—though it would still be quite good.

Suddenly, the copier started firing copies into the air. It sounded sort of like a machine gun.

It was just plain good luck that at that very moment Moxy's dream was turning from a good dream into a bad dream. She was still dreaming she was Eleanor Roosevelt, but her husband, who was the President of the United States, had just told her she had to write thank-you notes to every citizen in America for their help in the War Effort.

She was quite relieved, then, when a copy of one of her thank-you notes drifted onto her face and woke her.

Moxy took the note off her face and read it over. "Oh, good job!" she said.

By now the air was thick with flying thank-you notes. They covered the floor like big, flat snowflakes.

Here is a photograph Mark took of the thank-you notes as they shot out of the copier.

"That's all right," Moxy called back. "I can always use extras for birthdays and half birthdays, that sort of thing."

Moxy lay back on Ajax's La-Z-Boy. Somewhere between being Eleanor Roosevelt and being Moxy Maxwell, an important thought had occurred to her. But she couldn't remember what it was.

Then Granny George came over and covered Moxy's face with an afghan.

"How's your cold?" asked Granny George.

"It's an absolute misery," replied Moxy. Even though Moxy didn't have a cold, sometimes it was easier to go along with what Granny George thought was going on.

chapter 43
Moxy Suddenly Remembers What She Almost Forgot

"You guys, there's no 'Thank You' written on the outside of these thank-you notes!" cried Moxy.

You really couldn't hear her, though. Here's why:

1. There was the vibration of the copier.

2. There was the sound of each thank-you note being launched into the room at the rate of one every 11 seconds (as Mark calculated it).

3. There was the fact that Moxy's mouth was covered with an afghan.

"Would you like soup or would you like to starve?" asked Granny George. Granny George was always forgetting whether you were supposed to feed a cold and starve a fever or the other way around.

chapter 44
In Which Moxy
Takes Action

Slowly, very slowly, Moxy climbed onto the arm of Ajax's chair. She held the afghan over her head to protect her face from flying thank-you notes and then she jumped.

Here is a picture Mark took of Moxy jumping off the arm of Ajax's chair with the afghan covering her face. He called it "She Walks! She Talks! She Even Flies! No, She Doesn't."

"She Walks! She Talks! She Even Flies! No, She Doesn't," by Mark Maxwell.

Moxy landed on a nineteen-inch pile of Important Papers and slid around for a while. ("I might have been seriously injured," she said to her mother some days later.)

Then she followed Granny George into the kitchen.

chapter 45
In Which Moxy First Says the Words "Gold Spray Paint"

"Chicken noodle? Chicken and rice? Chicken and stars? Stars and stripes?" Granny George was getting out the saucepan.

"Do you know what would make me feel better?" said Moxy. "That can of gold spray paint." She pointed to Granny's crafts corner.

"For your cold?" said Granny George.

"For my new thank-you notes."

Granny George looked confused.

"I need to spray-paint 'Thank You' on the front of each one."

Granny George continued to look confused.

"Wait here," said Moxy. She ran upstairs, her afghan trailing after.

chapter 46
In Which Pansy Wanders into the Kitchen and Asks Granny George Where Moxy Is

Pansy wandered into the kitchen.

"Where's Moxy?" she said.

"Split-pea?" said Granny George.

"No, Moxy," repeated Pansy.

"Here I am." Moxy twirled into the kitchen, the afghan wrapped around her shoulders like a mink stole, and gave Granny George one of the thank-you notes from the box of thank-you notes her mother had given her.

"See what I mean?" said Moxy. "There's this big gold 'Thank You' written on the front. Now look at the thank-you notes I'm making." Moxy picked up one of the notes that had recently flown out of Ajax's office and landed on the kitchen floor. "There's no gold writing on these."

chapter 47
In Which Moxy Says the Words "Gold Spray Paint" Again

"Which is why," continued Moxy, "I need the gold spray paint. So I can spray-paint 'Thank You' on the front of each one. Otherwise they won't look like the ones Mom bought for me."

Pansy was confused, but Granny George understood. "Here's the gold spray paint," she said.

Pansy couldn't hide her surprise. "But you're not allowed."

"Granny George just said I could." Moxy smiled and began to shake the can.

Moxy loved the sound of the ball rattling inside. It felt like she was getting something done before she'd even started. She also loved the smell. But she wasn't supposed to smell it. In fact, Pansy was right: Moxy wasn't allowed to touch another can of spray paint until she was twenty-one.

chapter 48

5 Reasons Moxy Isn't Allowed to Touch Another Can of Spray Paint Until She's Twenty-one

Mark took this close-up picture of the list of reasons Moxy wasn't allowed to touch another can of spray paint until she was twenty-one. This list has been sealed to the refrigerator door (with the aid of spilled grape juice and a magnet that says THE VOLVO DOCTOR MAKES HOUSE CALLS!) for just over a year now—ever since Moxy's mother made Moxy write it.

Here is the picture Mark took of it.

chapter 49
In Which Moxy Keeps On Shaking the Can

But Moxy kept on shaking the can.

"Pansy," she said, "I need eleven more copies of my new thank-you notes."

Pansy disappeared into Ajax's office. As she went in, another thank-you note flew out.

"Moxy's going to use the gold spray paint," Pansy announced to Mark and Sam.

Mark wrapped his camera back around his neck and rushed into the kitchen.

Pansy, however, was not in a terrific hurry to go back. Even though she had liked being a princess, which was the reason they had spray-painted her hair gold in the first place, she had not liked the haircut that followed it. It was too short, for one thing— one person had even thought she was a boy.

That was a long time ago, of course— back when Moxy was nine and hadn't had much experience with spray paint.

chapter 50
3 Things Experience Has Taught Moxy About Gold Spray Paint

Now, Moxy knew a good deal more than the average ten-year-old about the uses and abuses of spray paint. Such as:

1. A little spray paint goes a long way.

2. Always put something you don't care about behind the thing you are spray-painting in case the spray paint misses its target.

3. Don't spray-paint your sister's hair.

As she shook the can (she did love the sound of that ball), Moxy mulled over the second rule. It meant she would have to lean the thank-you notes against something that wouldn't be ruined if she accidentally missed her target.

It occurred to her that the Christmas tree might be the perfect thing to lean the thank-you notes against while she spray-painted "Thank You" on the front of them. It was, after all, almost time to throw the tree out anyway. The tree was also almost dead. Plus it had gold ornaments on it, which meant that if a little gold spray paint accidentally hit the tree, it would hardly be noticed.

The plan had one small flaw: How would the thank-you notes stay on the tree while Moxy spray-painted them? She was wrestling with this problem when Granny George's cell phone began to play "Rock Around the Clock."

It was Uncle Jayne. His car was stuck in slush and other snow-related stuff and he would be there soon but not right away.

"He's going to walk over," Granny George told Moxy after she hung up.

But Moxy wasn't listening.

chapter 51
In Which Moxy (Once Again) Saves the Day

"Thank goodness I'm me," said Moxy. "Otherwise where would we be?"

"Pansy!" Moxy called.

There was no reply.

"Pansy!" Moxy called again. Pansy always came when Moxy called—but not this time. This time she stayed in Ajax's office.

"PANSY!" Moxy called for the third and final time. But Pansy didn't appear.

chapter 52
In Which Moxy Is Forced to Stop What She's Doing and Look for Pansy

If I were *Pansy and I thought I was a turtle, where would I look for me?* wondered Moxy.

Moxy looked everywhere she could think of for her sister —in both of the bathtubs and under all the beds. Finally, she tried Ajax's office. There she found both of Pansy's feet and what looked like part of her elbow under Ajax's chair. The rest of Pansy was covered in thank-you notes—and the copier was still firing away.

Here is the photograph Mark took of Pansy's feet. Note the untied shoes.

Both of Pansy Maxwell's feet.

Moxy shouted to Sam to turn off the copier. "I think I have enough thank-you notes now," she added.

chapter 53
In Which Pansy
Starts to Sort of Cry

Moxy very politely invited Pansy into the living room. She also invited her to stand in front of the Christmas tree and hold the thank-you notes while Moxy spray-painted "Thank You" on them.

But Pansy started to sort of cry.

"I'm not allowed," she sort of cried.

More than anyone, Sam understood why Pansy was sort of crying. He couldn't imagine saying no to Moxy.

Which was why he said yes when Moxy turned to him and asked if *he* would hold the thank-you notes in front of the Christmas tree while she spray-painted "Thank You" on them.

Naturally, Sam didn't want to leave the copier unattended. But since he couldn't figure out how to turn it off, he decided it didn't make much difference whether he stood in front of the copier that he couldn't turn off or in front of the Christmas tree holding a thank-you note while Moxy shot gold spray paint at him.

So Sam followed Moxy into the living room.

chapter 54
The First Shot

Here's a picture Mark took of Sam holding a thank-you note in front of the Christmas tree while Moxy continued to shake the gold spray paint. He called it "BEFORE."

Dear _____,

Thank you for _____ very _____ . It is _____ and it will come in handy. I'll use it for various things like _____ . In case you want to thank me for this thank you note, please wait until I get back from visiting my dad in Hollywood. I will be there for 6½ days.

Have a breath-taking New Year!

Love,
Moxy Anne Maxwell

"BEFORE," by Mark Maxwell.

Moxy closed her right eye. She took careful aim. She changed her mind. Maybe she was supposed to close her left eye and keep her right eye open. The eye doctor who had told her she didn't need glasses had also told her that one eye was stronger than the other. But she couldn't remember which was which. So she stood there closing one eye and then the other for so long that Sam thought he might faint, and Moxy started to get a headache.

Finally, she just sprayed away.

Here is the picture Mark took of Sam when Moxy was through spray-painting him.

"AFTER," by Mark Maxwell.

It is obvious to even the casual viewer why Mark called this the "after" photograph. You don't need glasses to see the big gold "T" on Sam's new red Christmas shirt.

Granted, Sam was a little surprised to look down and see the big gold "T." But, as Moxy pointed out, it did look like he had just gotten a letter for achievement in sports—kind of.

chapter 55
The Big "HANK YOU"

While Pansy and Sam were admiring Sam's new shirt, Moxy was staring at the big "HANK YOU" she had just sprayed on the living room wall beside the Christmas tree. I can't describe Moxy's expression, but Mark took this picture of her so you can see for yourself:

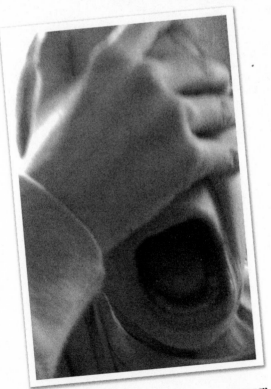

Moxy Maxwell first sees the big "HANK YOU."

And here is a picture Mark took of the big "HANK YOU" looking at Moxy.

The big "HANK YOU" looks at Moxy.

chapter 56
In Which Mrs. Maxwell Walks in the Door Carrying a Cute Little Pink Dress with Gobs of Glitter for Moxy to Wear to the Big New Year's Eve Star-Studded Hollywood Bash Her Father Is Taking Her To

"I'm home," called Mrs. Maxwell.

There was no answer.

"Uncle Jayne? Granny George?" she called.

Then she sniffed the air. "Is that spray paint I smell? Granny George, are you making more bracelets out of tuna fish cans?"

Granny George had just developed a new product: she took the top and bottom off tuna fish cans (even though sometimes they were still full of tuna and no one was in the mood for a tuna fish sandwich), spray-painted them gold, and turned them into big gold bracelets to sell at the annual Save the Ivory-billed Woodpecker Fund-raiser.

Mrs. Maxwell stayed in the hall stomping her boots. Granny George came out to greet her.

"He's stuck in slush," said Granny George.

"Uncle Jayne is stuck in slush?" asked Mrs. Maxwell.

"His car is stuck in slush. He went home to put the turkey in," Granny George explained.

"He did the right thing," said Mrs. Maxwell. She would never forget the turkey Aunt Margaret had made last Thanksgiving—it had been such an odd shade of gray.

chapter 57
In Which
Mrs. Maxwell Asks
What That Noise Is

"What's that noise?" called Mrs. Maxwell.

There was a general silence.

Then Mark wandered into the hall with his camera, looking for a photo op. He knew something big was afoot.

chapter 58
The Case of the Flying Thank-you Notes

"What's this?" said Mrs. Maxwell. She picked a blue thank-you note up off the floor. But her gloves were wet and it turned soggy right away. Another blue thank-you note flew by.

"Would someone please read that to me?" said Mrs. Maxwell pleasantly.

Granny George picked it up and passed it to Mark. Mark carefully placed his camera in Granny George's hands and rapidly read the note out loud.

"Dear-Thank-you-for-It-is-very-and-it-will-come-in-handy-I'll-use-it-for-various-things-like-and-In-case-you-want-to-thank-me-for-this-thank-you-note-please-wait-until-I-get-back-from-visiting-my-dad-in-Hollywood-I-will-be-there-for-six-and-a-half-days-Have-a-breathtaking-New-Year-Love-Moxy-Anne-Maxwell."

chapter 59
In Which Mrs. Maxwell Calls Out (and Not for the First Time in Her Life), "Moxy Anne Maxwell!"

"Moxy Anne Maxwell!"

Moxy figured there was too much noise for her to hear her mother calling out her name, so she didn't reply.

When Moxy didn't reply, Mrs. Maxwell marched into the living room to find her. (Have you noticed how mothers always seem to *march* into rooms when you don't answer right away?)

chapter 60

In Which We Linger with Mrs. Maxwell to Give Moxy a Chance to Think of an Explanation for This Mess

As soon as she saw the big "HANK YOU" spray-painted on her living room wall, Mrs. Maxwell collapsed onto the sofa and put her head between her knees and tried to breathe.

Here is the photograph Mark took of Mrs. Maxwell trying to breathe.

Mrs. Maxwell is somewhere in there with her head between her knees.

It was touch and go—Sam and Pansy thought she might faint. Mark was pretty sure she wouldn't. Moxy didn't have an opinion one way or the other.

That's because she was busy rocking in the rocking chair—which was where she did some of her best thinking.

chapter 61

In Which We Take a Chapter Off to Give Moxy a Little More Time to Think of an Explanation for This Mess

chapter 62
In Which the Unasked Question—"How could things get worse?"— Is Answered

You may have been wondering how things could get worse.

Well, Ajax could walk in the front door.

chapter 63
In Which Ajax Walks in the Front Door

Ajax walked in the front door.

"What's that noise?" he said to no one. Ajax often asked himself questions out loud. In this case, he already knew the answer: It was the sound of his new Christmas copier— the one *nobody* was supposed to touch.

Ajax didn't stop to take off his snowy coat and boots. He didn't look left or right. He walked right past the big "HANK YOU" sprayed in gold on the green wall—right past Mrs. Maxwell sitting in a heap with her head between her knees. He was following the flying blue thank-you notes.

chapter 64
Mrs. Maxwell Asks an Obvious Question

Mrs. Maxwell lifted her head from between her knees. "What on earth is going on here?" she said.

"I'm writing my thank-you notes," Moxy explained patiently.

Mrs. Maxwell raised her head a bit higher and took a good look around. "On the living room wall?"

chapter 65
In Which the Copier Stops and Ajax Sits in His Broken La-Z-Boy

After he turned off his new Christmas copier, Ajax waded through 473 thank-you notes (Mark counted them later), accidentally stepping on a 21-inch pile of Important Papers as he went. Then he sighed, sank into his La-Z-Boy chair, and pulled the lever to bring the back up so he could take a better look around.

But the back didn't come up. It stayed flat on its back.

Then Ajax said to the copier and to the broken chair and to us, the reading

129

audience, "Grown men don't cry," and a pair of tears strolled down his left cheek.

He eased himself all the way back into his broken favorite chair and stared at the ceiling.

The ceiling could use a coat of paint, he thought.

chapter 66
In Which Ajax Takes the Temperature of His New Christmas Copier

Ajax spent several minutes trying to figure out how his office had turned into such an impressive mess in such a short time. He had only gone out to buy eggnog and the *Paris Review,* and yes, okay, on the way home he *had* stopped at the library to see if they had ordered his most recent book, and while he was there he *had* run into his best friend, Ted Bear, and it's true, they'd gotten a cup of coffee—or two—and discussed the future of children's literature.

But still and all, and all in all, he hadn't been gone *that* long.

Ajax struggled out of the chair, crossed the room to his new Christmas copier, and took its temperature with his hand. (It was quite hot.) Then he wandered back into the living room.

chapter 67
In Which Ajax Uses His Powers of Observation

Right away Ajax noticed that there was something different about the living room. But what? He stood there thinking about it. Then his Powers of Observation kicked in.

"Why does that wall say 'HANK YOU'?" he said.

"Well, it's the funniest thing," said Moxy.

But no one laughed, although Granny George looked hopeful, as if she were waiting to be told a good joke.

"You see, I had this brilliant idea," Moxy began again.

She waited, but no one asked what her brilliant idea was.

"Does anyone want to know what my brilliant idea was?"

Granny George raised her hand.

Mark took this picture of her:

"Since you asked, I'll tell you," Moxy went on. "My brilliant idea was to save scads of time on my thank-you notes by writing 'Dear' and 'Thank you for whatever' and 'Love, Moxy' on one piece of paper and then making copies of it."

"You know you're not allowed to touch Ajax's new copier. *And*," added Mrs. Maxwell, "I *know* you know you're not allowed to touch another can of spray paint until you're twenty-one. It says so on the refrigerator."

"But it was for the Greater Good, Mother."

"Who is the Greater Good?" asked Pansy.

"It's not a person," said Moxy. *But what exactly is it?* Moxy asked herself. She couldn't quite remember.

"The Greater Good means . . . it has something to do with the fact . . . and so, which is why . . ."

chapter 68
The Greater Good Explained

Moxy looked at Mark. Mark had taught her the phrase. He even knew what it meant. (Mark could have belonged to Mensa, which is a country club for geniuses, but he thought it was stupid.)

"Mark," said Moxy, yawning, "would you please explain to everyone what 'the Greater Good' is? I'm feeling a bit tired."

"It means you do something you know is wrong in order to achieve something that is more important than the wrong thing is wrong."

"And so, as you can see and in conclusion, that is why I was forced to break a couple of rules." Moxy glanced at the gold "T" on Sam's shirt and the big "HANK YOU" on the green wall.

"What could be more important than obeying the Spray-Paint Rules?" said Mrs. Maxwell. Mrs. Maxwell was quite calm. But those of you who are familiar with Mrs. Maxwell from other stories know that when Mrs. Maxwell is quite calm, she is actually quite the opposite.

"Getting my thank-you notes done was more important—so I can go see Dad in Hollywood." It was so obvious. Moxy didn't understand why her mother had to ask.

chapter 69
In Which Moxy Maxwell Learns What the Phrase "Saved by the Bell" Means

"Saved by the bell" means your mother's cell phone rings just as she is about to yell at you.

Mrs. Maxwell's cell phone was playing the second round of "You Are the Sunshine of My Life" when she finally found it in the hall under her black winter coat in her caramel brown purse. It was wet, but she answered it anyway.

"Hello?" was all anyone heard her say before she drifted into Ajax's study so she could have some privacy.

chapter 70
A One-way Phone Conversation

Mrs. Maxwell was so involved in her phone conversation, she hardly noticed the mess in Ajax's office. Nor did she notice that Mark was in the office too. He was behind Ajax's broken chair counting thank-you notes.

Because Mark could only hear his mother's side of the conversation, we can only hear his mother's side of the conversation.

The first thing Mrs. Maxwell said into her cell phone was "What did you say?"

This was followed by a 31-second pause—Mark timed it—while the other person talked.

Then Mrs. Maxwell said, "Do you know how long they've been looking forward to this?"

This was followed by a 134-second pause while the other person talked.

Then Mrs. Maxwell said, "No deal on earth is more important than seeing your children."

This was followed by a 17-second pause.

Then Mrs. Maxwell said, "Mark and Moxy *are* the biggest deals of your life. And no, I don't care if the entire Old Testament is never made into a miniseries."

Then Mrs. Maxwell hung up.

Then Mrs. Maxwell stared at the ceiling.

That ceiling could use a coat of paint, she thought.

As soon as his mother left the room, Mark leaned his head against the right arm of Ajax's broken La-Z-Boy chair and tried not to cry.

chapter 71
In Which Moxy Forgives Her Mother

"Mother, you're looking pale. Why don't you sit down?" said Moxy when her mother came back into the living room.

For the first time that day, Moxy and her mother agreed.

Mrs. Maxwell sat on the sofa.

"The gold spray paint on this wall"— Moxy gestured behind her—"and on Sam's new red Christmas shirt is not entirely your fault."

"I'm relieved to hear it," said Mrs. Maxwell.

Moxy could tell that her mother wasn't really listening.

"The thing is, if you hadn't given me thank-you notes that said 'Thank You' on the front in big gold letters, I wouldn't have been forced to spray-paint 'Thank You' on the notes I made with Ajax's copier, and"— Moxy finished her little speech in a hurry— "and the wall wouldn't say 'HANK YOU.' "

"I see," said Mrs. Maxwell.

"Oh, Mother, I knew you would!" Moxy was too tired to jump up and hug her mother. "And I promise, the very second Mark and I get back from Hollywood, Sam and Pansy will paint the living room wall."

When her mother didn't reply, Moxy added, "Not just that wall—all the walls. In fact, this whole place could use some fresh paint. I noticed Ajax's ceiling was . . ."

Mrs. Maxwell couldn't bring herself to look at Moxy.

"And," added Moxy, "I promise I'll finish all my thank-you notes while I'm in Hollywood. Dad will help me."

Moxy could tell from her mother's expression—she was sort of staring at the wall that didn't say "HANK YOU" on it—that she *still* wasn't paying attention.

"Guess what else I'll do? I'll make Dad buy stamps and we'll *actually mail* every single thank-you note right from Hollywood."

chapter 72
In Which
Mrs. Maxwell Ruins
Moxy's Life

"I'm so sorry," said Mrs. Maxwell gently, "but you won't be able to mail your thank-you notes from Hollywood. I'm afraid you're not going to be able to go."

"I am too," said Moxy.

"No, you see—"

"I told you I was sorry!" interrupted Moxy. She thought for a moment. "Didn't I?" She wasn't sure. "Well, I am." Now her throat was sore with backed-up tears. "I can't disappoint Dad. I promised I would be his escort at the Big New Year's Eve Star-Studded Hollywood Bash."

"It's more complicated than that," said Mrs. Maxwell. "You see, your dad . . ." Mrs. Maxwell stopped talking. She knew how much Moxy adored her father.

"My dad *what*?"

"Will probably miss you, but—"

"But what?"

"But there's always next year."

"*This is so unfair*—I haven't seen him in almost three whole years! Plus Mark will be afraid to fly on a jumbo jet without me. Right, Mark?"

Quite unexpectedly, Mark said, "Yes."

"See? It's not fair to Mark either." Moxy wiped some tears into her elbow. "I said I was sorry for everything. I'm even sorry I was born."

Moxy ran into the hallway. She paused for a moment at the foot of the stairs, hoping her mother would change her mind.

But her mother stayed silent, and finally, Moxy started to sob.

Then she ran upstairs and collapsed on her bed.

chapter 73
In Which Moxy Realizes Her Life Is Over

Moxy's life was over. It was as simple as that. Gone were the 17 starving children from all over the world. Gone was her chance to be a rich and famous but very nice movie star. Her private tour of Universal Studios—gone. The screen test her father was going to set up for her—not going to happen. Now she would never stand in Johnny Depp's footprints at Grauman's Chinese Theatre; never stand on the stage of the Hollywood Bowl and belt out "Tomorrow." Tomorrow her father would not be waiting to pick her up at the airport in his powder blue convertible stretch limo. Moxy didn't care if tomorrow never came.

chapter 74
In Which Moxy
Doesn't Stop Crying

Moxy fell asleep before she had a chance to stop crying.

When she woke, it was dark. But the lights that lit up the backyard were on, and she could see snow starting to fall. The smell of what must have been turkey soup was nestled in her room. It made her hungry.

The clock said it was 11:15 p.m., which meant she had been asleep for 6 hours and 10 minutes and her mother still hadn't knocked on her door to say she had changed her mind about letting Moxy go to Hollywood.

Moxy hated, hated, hated her mother. She hated her more than she had ever hated her—not that she had really and truly ever hated her before.

chapter 75
In Which Mark Knocks on Moxy's Door

Moxy heard a knock. She knew it was Mark by the muffled sound of it. Mark had always been a quiet knocker.

"Don't come in," said Moxy.

Mark came in and sat on the edge of Moxy's other bed. He looked down at his feet. "What's up?" he said.

"Except for the fact that my life is over?"

Moxy tried to cry again, but apparently she was out of tears.

"I hate Mom," said Moxy.

Mark started looking through the view-finder of his camera at the pictures he'd taken.

"It's not her fault," he muttered.

"I *know*. But you'd think she'd forgive me *this one time* so we could go to Hollywood. She knows how much this trip means to us."

"Speak for yourself," said Mark. He was looking at the picture he'd taken of Moxy modeling her long black evening gown for the Big New Year's Eve Star-Studded Hollywood Bash.

Moxy went over and sat beside him.

"Black becomes me—don't you agree?" said Moxy, looking at her glamorous self over Mark's shoulder.

"I guess so."

"You *really* don't want to see Dad?"

Mark clicked to the picture he'd taken of Granny George's legs.

"Dad doesn't want to see me," said Mark.

"Of course he does! He invited us both."

"Well, now he's uninvited us," said Mark without looking up.

"But Dad wouldn't do that. He *promised* that *this* year we could come for Christmas."

"He promised we could come for Christmas *last* year too."

"But last year a Very Big Deal came up at the last minute," said Moxy.

Mark looked up. "And *this* year a Very Big Deal came up at the last minute too."

"What?" Moxy was astonished. "*This* year a Very Big Deal came up? How do you know?"

"I heard Mom talking to Dad on her cell phone."

chapter 76
A Marvelous Thing

Mark went to the window.

"But Mom would have told us if Dad was the one who canceled the trip. She always tells the truth," said Moxy.

"I guess she didn't want to hurt our feelings," said Mark.

Moxy thought about it.

She couldn't believe her mother would take the blame for the fact that they couldn't go to Hollywood when it was really her dad's fault.

Then Mark took this picture through

Moxy's bedroom window of the little white twinkling lights he and Ajax had wrapped around the trees and bushes on the first day of Christmas vacation.

The little white twinkling lights.

When he put his camera down, Mark's eyes were sparkling with tears.

Moxy went over and stood at the window beside him. The snow was starting to get thick now. Together they watched as the snow began to blur the little white lights.

"I'm sorry," she said.

Mark looked at Moxy.

"It's no *Big Deal*," he replied. Then he started to grin.

"What's so funny?"

"It's no *Big Deal*," repeated Mark, "but it *would* be to Dad."

It took a second, and then Moxy started to laugh.

She wasn't sure why she was laughing. When she thought about it, things couldn't have been worse—except they didn't feel *that* bad.

For one thing, even if her dad didn't have time to take her to the Big New Year's Eve

Star-Studded Hollywood Bash this year, it didn't mean she couldn't keep the new pink gobs-of-glitter dress her mother had brought back from the mall—in fact, she could wear it to her Debut Piano Recital on April 23!

And another thing: There was the distinct possibility her mother would feel sorry enough for her to grant a thank-you-note extension till, say, Martin Luther King's Birthday or even Groundhog Day.

And wasn't her mother kind of marvelous for taking the blame for the fact that Moxy and Mark couldn't go to Hollywood? "Marvelous" was a word Moxy had recently learned. But she'd been saving it to use until something really and truly marvelous came along.

"Good night," said Mark.

"Good night back," said Moxy, even though she wasn't going to sleep.

Then Moxy crawled into bed and turned on her little red reading light and pulled her favorite comforter that smelled a little like Pine-Sol and a little like Chanel No. 5 over her head and began to write the first real thank-you note of her life.

Just before he closed the door, Mark took this picture of her:

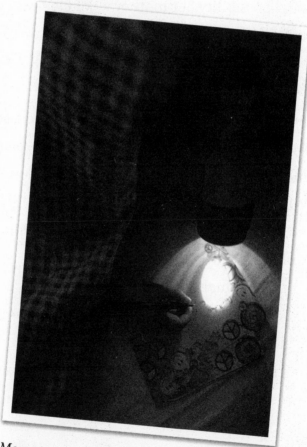

Moxy starts to write the first real thank-you note of her life.

chapter 77
Mrs. Maxwell Has Christmas Again

When Mrs. Maxwell got up the next morning, she found this note under her door.

Here is what Moxy wrote:

Dear Mother,

Thank you for loving me so much.

Have a breath-taking New Year!

Love,

Moxy Anne Maxwell

(Your daughter)

P.S. In case you want to thank me for this thank you note, I'll be around all week.

And here is the picture Moxy made Mark

take of it so she would have her own copy of what she called her "first literary master-piece."

About the Author

Peggy Gifford is the author of *Moxy Maxwell Does Not Love* Stuart Little, which reviewers have lauded as "irresistibly authentic," "wildly original," and "unforgettable." She holds an MFA from the Iowa Writers' Workshop and has worked as an editor for the Feminist Press and as an acquisitions editor for SUNY Press. Peggy divides her time between New York City and South Carolina with her husband, Jack. You can visit Peggy and Moxy at www.peggy gifford.com.

About the Illustrator

Valorie Fisher is the author and illustrator of several books, including *When Ruby Tried to Grow Candy, How High Can a Dinosaur Count?, My Big Brother,* and *Ellsworth's Extraordinary Electric Ears.* Her photographs for *Moxy Maxwell Does Not Love* Stuart Little have been called "fresh," "spot-on," "funny," and "snort-inducing." Valorie's photographs can be seen in the collections of major museums around the world, including the Brooklyn Museum, London's Victoria and Albert Museum, and the Bibliothèque Nationale in Paris. She lives in Cornwall, Connecticut, with her husband and their two children.